I Can Read! ZONDERkidz

BEGINNING 1 READING

The Berenstain Bears
Faith Gets Us Through

Story and Pictures By

Stan & Jan Berenstain with Mike Berenstain

Living Lights

D0037460

Today was a special day.

The Bear Scouts were going to

Spooky Cave.

They wanted to earn their

Cave Adventure Merit Badges.

Scout Sister said, "I am a little scared."

4

Scout Brother said, "Me, too."

Scout Fred said, "As the Bible says,

'The Lord is my light and my salvation

—whom shall I fear?'"

Spooky Cave looked spooky!

It looked like a big, open mouth

with big, sharp teeth.

Scout Papa said, "Come on, scouts.

Don't be scared.

All we need is a little faith.

Let's earn those badges."

Mountain goats watched Papa

and the scouts go into the cave.

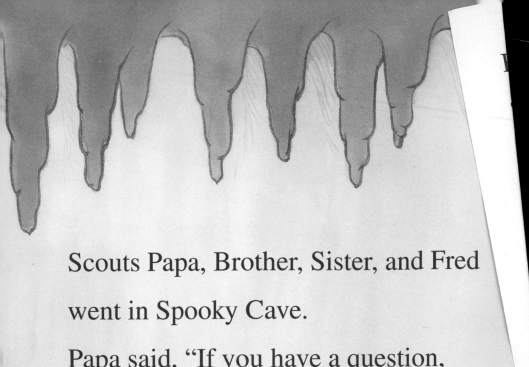

Scouts Papa, Brother, Sister, and Fred
went in Spooky Cave.
Papa said, "If you have a question,
just ask me.
I know all about caves."
Sister asked,
"What are these pointy things?"

red said,
'Some of those pointy
things grow up and
some grow down."

Papa said, "Yes. Listen to this rhyme—
Stalactites and stalagmites,

Only caves got 'em.

Tites are up on top.

Mites are on the bottom."

The scouts looked up.

They looked down.

God made amazing things!

Then Sister said,

"It sounds funny in the cave."

Papa said, "I know all about caves,

so let me tell you.

It sounds funny because there is an

echo in the cave.

Listen."

Papa shouted, "HELLO!"

The scouts heard the sound bounce

off the cave walls.

'HELLO! Hello! Hello!'

went the echo.

But Papa forgot that noises in
a cave can shake things loose.

"Be strong and courageous,"
Fred quoted from the Bible.
"And look out!"

"YIPE!" said Papa.

A falling stalactite just missed him!

Papa and the scouts went
deeper into the cave.
The scouts said a prayer to
keep up their courage.

Soon, they could not
remember which
way they had
come.

Sister asked, "Are we lost?"

Papa said, "We are not lost.

I know all about caves so

I left a trail of string."

But Papa did not know a goat

had followed them.

The goat had eaten the trail of string.

The scouts asked, "What will we do?"

Papa said, "Never fear!

I know all about caves."

Papa got his finger wet. He held it up.

"I feel a breeze," said Papa.

"That means there is another way out."

But Papa did not know about

the stream in Spooky Cave.

"Yiiieee!" shouted Papa, as he fell in the water.

"Lord, help us!" prayed the scouts.

Down,

down

they went.

Down,

down,

down …

… and out of

Spooky Cave.

God kept them safe.
The scouts were
back outside!

Papa said, "Here are your Cave
Adventure Merit Badges."

Fred said, "Our faith and prayers
sure helped us get through."

Sister said, "It was fun."

Brother said, "Just like a water slide."

"Scout Papa, may we go back
in the cave?" Fred asked.

Papa said, "Scouts, I know all about caves.
I am glad you asked that question.
The answer is …

But the scouts were happy.

They were happy they had faith.

They were happy they had their badges.

They were happy Papa knew

everything about caves.

Well ...

almost everything.